The Dragon That Wanted To Play In The Snow

by Kate and Ricardo Balderas

Illustrated by Don Berry

Printed in China by Global PSD
ISBN 1-59457-172-4

We dedicate this book to children everywhere.

Love,

Kate and Ricardo

Not long ago,
but quite far away,
lived a sad little dragon
in a house that was gray.

It wasn't gray by color,
the outside was quite bright.
The grayness was in Dragon's heart.
He just never got things right.

Now his problem seemed big
and his problem seemed huge.
For whatever he began,
he'd eventually lose.

Not like you're thinking
when something can't be found,
but burned to a crisp,
and that's why he'd frown.

Every time Dylan the Dragon would talk,
he'd breathe fire you see.
Even burn off his socks!

Now singeing his clothes
isn't what made him so sad.
It was bigger than that
which made him feel bad.

In the woods where he lived
in his little gray house,
it snowed all year long
but he couldn't go out.

For all of his friends asked him,
"please do not play,
for whenever you breathe,
our snow melts away."

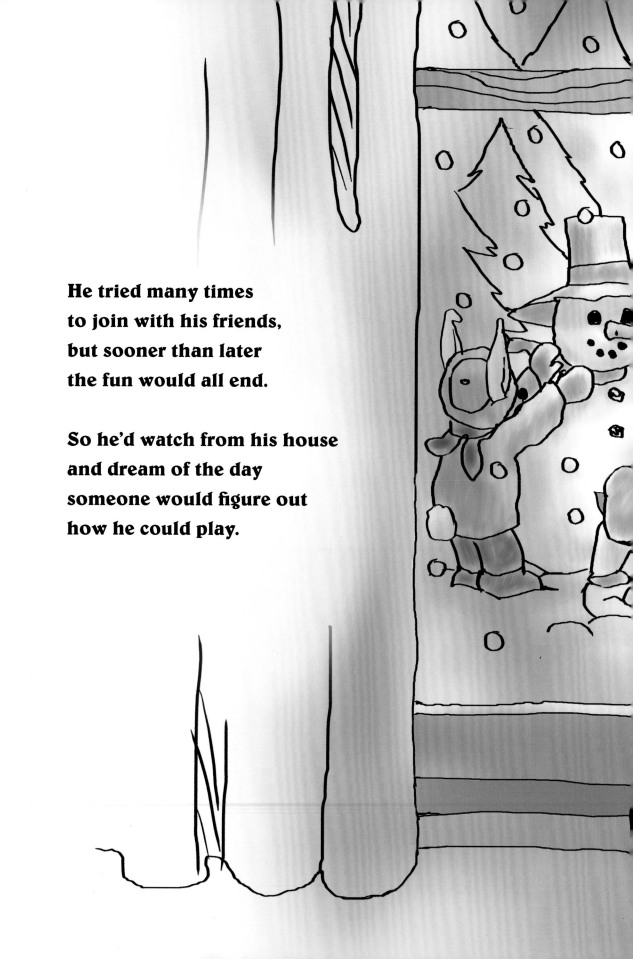

He tried many times
to join with his friends,
but sooner than later
the fun would all end.

So he'd watch from his house
and dream of the day
someone would figure out
how he could play.

Now Dylan's best friend
lived close by in a tree,
a little gray squirrel
who was named Katie Bee.

She would sit in his window,
for hours they'd talk
and go shopping for Dylan
and bring him new socks.

DRAGON SOCKS FIREPROOF!

But her dream of all dreams
was to help her dear friend,
to play in the snow
from beginning to end.

She'd think and she'd think
and she'd think once again.
"I just have to help Dylan
for he's my best friend."

Then one night in bed
in Katie Bee's sleep,
she dreamed of a way
to turn down Dylan's heat.

Auntie Irma had sent,
just a few days ago,
some beautiful earmuffs
to play in the snow.

What if she gave them
to Dylan instead,
to place on his nose
and not on his head?

With a few tucks here
and some extra tucks there,
those small little muffs
would fit even a bear

Now Dylan was jumping
from the ground to the trees,
free to play in the snow
for as long as he pleased.

He never ever wanted
to make fire again.
He'd just live in the snow
and play with his friends.

Until one night in winter
about Christmas Eve,
there hit the biggest blizzard
anyone had ever seen.

The snow was so thick
it was so cold in their town,
that the houses and trees
were turned upside and down.

But worse than that
and sad as can be,
Dylan searched and searched,
but no Katie Bee.

The tree that she lived in
was nowhere to be found.
The street lights and roads
disappeared without sound.

The town folk met
in the ice and the snow,
"We must find some heat.
Oh, where shall we go?"

Then Dylan thought
of the flames he could make
by removing the muffs
he had placed on his face.

"I can help, I can help "
Dylan said with a puff.
"I can get us all warm
if I take off these muffs."

He took a deep breath
and then one breath more,
and the warmth of his fire
came out with a roar.

His friends found a tree
blown down by the snow,
and with one mighty puff
Dylan's breath made it glow.

Now next to this tree
yet another one lay,
and inside a hole
sat a squirrel that was gray.

"Katie Bee, Katie Bee "
Dylan cried with delight,
"I've found you my friend
with my fire so bright."

The animals cheered,
they had hope once again,
thanks to Dylan the Dragon
their fire-breathing friend.

The mayor of the village
said with delight,
"We'd be honored to have
your fire each night,

light the lanterns along
the streets of our town."
While Katie Bee noticed
there was no more frown

left on Dylan the Dragon,
now filled with such pride,
for he knew the importance
of his gift from inside.

For Dylan had learned
he was special you see,
special like you
and special like me.

The End